FRED BEAR &

FIRST

Plane

TRIP

Copyright © ticktock Entertainment Ltd 2007
First published in Great Britain in 2007 by ticktock Media Ltd.,
Unit 2, Orchard Business Centre, North Farm Road,
Tunbridge Wells, Kent, TN2 3XF

author: Melanie Joyce
ticktock project editor: Julia Adams
ticktock project designer: Emma Randall
ticktock image co-ordinator: Lizzie Knowles

We would like to thank: Colin Beer, Tim Bones, Rebecca Clunes, James Powell, Dr. Naima Browne,
Sharon Wright and Virgin Atlantic, Faye Wiffen and the staff at Gatwick Airport, and Jo Oliver and the staff at Lydd Airport

ISBN 978 1 84696 508 1 pbk

Printed in China

Picture credits
t=top, b=bottom, c=centre, l=left, r=right, bg=background
All photography by Colin Beer of JL Allwork Photography except for the following: Airteam Images: 12-13, 17, 18l, 23br. Getty: 20 inset. Shutterstock: 11, 13 inset, 16r, 24tr, 24br.
Superstock: 15tl. Virgin International picture archive: 14, 23cl.

Every effort has been made to trace the copyright holders, and we apologise in advance for any unintentional omissions.
We would be pleased to insert the appropriate acknowledgements in any subsequent edition of this publication.

Meet Fred Bear and Friends

Fred

Arthur

Betty

Jess

Uncle George

Arrivals ✈→

Departures ✈↑

Check-in ←

Information ?i ↘

Fred Bear is going to visit Uncle George.

Fred has never been on a plane before. He is excited.

At the airport, all his friends say "Goodbye!"

5

Fred goes to the check-in desk. "Ticket and passport please," says the airline worker.

"Here is your boarding pass, Fred," the airline worker says.

The boarding pass shows Fred his seat number.

The airline worker takes Fred's suitcase.

Fred hears a voice through the loudspeaker: "All passengers please go to Gate 3".

Fred's plane is ready for boarding.

Fred is very excited. He can see the plane through the window.

"Wow!" says Fred,

"What an enormous plane."

Fred climbs up the steps to get on the plane.

Fred sits down on his seat. The plane is about to take off.

'Bing-bong' goes a bell.

Then a sign lights up, and a voice says:

"Please fasten your seatbelts."

The plane moves slowly at first.
Then it goes faster and faster until...

WHOOSH! The plane lifts up off the ground.

Fred looks out of the window. Down below cars and houses get smaller and smaller.

"We are very high up," says Fred.

Fred enjoys looking out of
the window.

"Look!" Fred says,

"we are above the clouds."

14

It is time for
lunch. Fred folds
out his table.

After lunch, Fred
does a puzzle
and listens to his
favourite story.

It is nearly
time to land.

'Bing-
bong,'

goes the
bell again.
The seatbelt
sign lights up.

Fred fastens
his seatbelt.

16

Fred Bear says...

When the plane is landing, you might get the feeling your ears are popping. Drinking and yawning, during the landing stops this feeling.

The plane is getting closer and closer to the ground.

Then the plane lands
on the runway...

Bumpety-bump!

When the plane stops,
Fred Bear climbs down
the big steps.

Fred Bear goes to collect his suitcase.

The luggage belt rumbles around. "There is my case!" says Fred.

Uncle George is waiting in Arrivals. Fred can't wait to tell him that planes are just **amazing!**

Fred Bear

Lo at the pictures
and pik the missing words.

When you go
on holiday you
pack your
clothes in a...?

(passport) (suitcase)

At the airport
you have to
show your...?

(ticket) (hands)

On the plane you sit...?

- on the floor
- in a seat

The plane flies high above the...?

- clouds
- windows

When it is time to come down, the plane lands on the...?

- runway
- grass

Help Fred Bear find his suitcase. Which coloured path leads to Fred's suitcase?

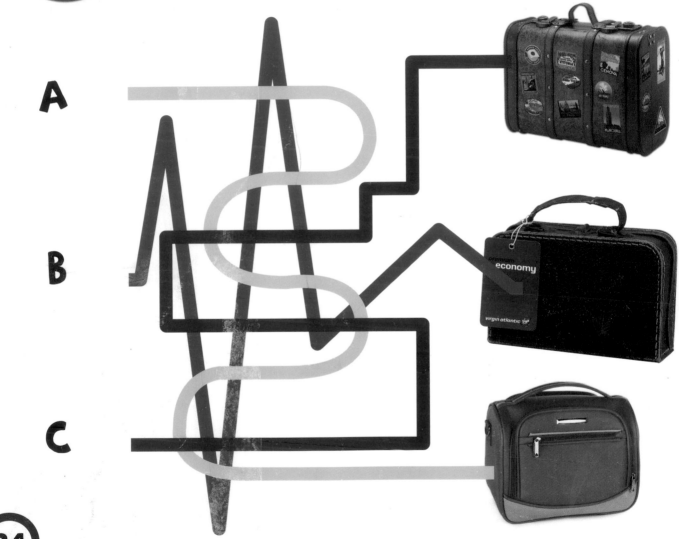

A

B

C

24